ECHOES OF ANXIETY

"Not every voice in your mind speaks the truth, some are echoes of fear."

By Bhoomika Madhusudan

Content

Preface

Anxiety can feel like an invisible force, holding you back, trapping you in your own thoughts, making the simplest tasks seem impossible. If you've ever felt this way, you're not alone. Anxiety is often misunderstood. Many see it as just nervousness, something that can be shaken off with a deep breath or a positive mindset. But those who live with it know the truth, anxiety is more than just worry. It's a constant battle within the mind, an overwhelming tide of thoughts that can make the simplest tasks feel impossible. It's the racing heartbeat before a conversation, the endless second-guessing after it, and the fear of judgment that turns everyday situations into unbearable challenges.

Too often, people mistake anxiety for weakness. They think it's something that can be "fixed" or "overcome" if only the person tried harder. But anxiety isn't a flaw in character, it's an invisible struggle that millions face, often in silence. This misunderstanding leaves many feelings alone, trapped within their own minds, believing that no one truly understands what they're going through.

That's why this book exists.

Through Adveet's journey, I want to take you inside the mind of someone who experiences anxiety first-hand. But this isn't just a story about struggle it's a story of understanding, growth, and hope. This book isn't about "curing" anxiety, because the truth is, anxiety doesn't always disappear. Instead, it's about learning to live with it, to navigate its challenges, and to stop letting it control your life.

You will see Adveet's fears, his doubts, and the way his mind builds obstacles that feel impossible to overcome. But you'll also see him learn, heal, and find the strength to move forward, not by eliminating anxiety, but by changing how he responds to it. His journey is a metaphor for what so many people experience in real life: the battle between intrusive thoughts and reality, the weight of perfectionism, and the realization that fear loses its power when we stop running from it.

If you have ever felt trapped by your own thoughts, if you've ever avoided something because of fear, or if you've ever wondered why your mind seems to work against you, this book is for you.

This is not just a story, it's a journey of self-discovery, resilience, and finding light in the darkest corners of the mind.

So, take a deep breath.

Let's begin.

[viii]

The Voices Within

Before beginning this journey, it is important to understand the key elements at play. Mental health is not just shaped by external experiences, it is deeply influenced by internal voices that guide, challenge, and sometimes hinder personal growth. These voices exist in this book are not imaginary they represent the voices exist in all of us, influencing the way we see the world and ourselves, representing different aspects of the human mind.

The Characters of the Mind

Cortic,

The overthinker, questions every step.

Critic

Echoes the weight of external judgment.

Echo

Traps us in the cycle of doubt, and then there is

Neuro,

The quiet guide, reminding us that growth is possible.

This story is a journey through these voices—the ones that hold us back and the ones that can set us free. Understanding them is the first step in taking control.

As you turn the page and embark on this journey, remember: **the mind is complex, but it is not the enemy. It is the key to resilience, self-acceptance, and healing.**

The Gathering

The cold winter air wrapped around the small town like a thick blanket, the streets dusted with fresh snow that crunched underfoot. Inside the grand old house at the end of the lane, warmth radiated from the crackling fireplace, filling the space with a comforting glow. The house, which had witnessed generations of love, laughter, and struggles, was now alive with the presence of family.

Grandparents, standing at the heart of the living room, their faces lined with age yet glowing with contentment, welcomed their loved ones with open arms. It was a special night; one they had long dreamed of. With their children, grandchildren, and even great-grandchildren gathered under one roof, they wanted to celebrate their journey and thanks giving party for the life they had built together.

Laughter echoed through the halls as relatives embraced, reconnecting after years apart. Conversations buzzed in every corner, memories being shared, stories of old rekindling forgotten emotions. The children played in joy, their giggles adding a musical charm to the evening. Everyone was wrapped in the warmth of togetherness. It was an evening of love, of bonds reaffirmed.

But amidst the joy, a sudden commotion broke through the celebration. A loud noise came from the corner of the room, followed by a frantic shuffle.

A lady's voice rang out in alarm, "Adveet!"

A teenage boy, barely seventeen, stood trembling, his breath quick and shallow. His chest rose and fell rapidly, his fingers clenched into tight fists. Panic flickered in his wide eyes as he struggled to breathe. His face turned pale, beads of sweat forming on his forehead despite the cold. The room fell silent as people turned towards him, concern washing over their faces.

He gasped for air, his hands clutching at his throat as though an invisible force was strangling him. His siblings rushed to his side; panic mirrored in their expressions.

His mother cried out, rushing forward, but before she could reach him, a calm yet firm voice cut through the silence.

A psychologist who was present in the gathering stepped in, her presence steady and reassuring. "Everyone, give him space," she instructed, guiding the boy gently to a quieter corner of the room with the help of his siblings. She spoke to him in a soft, steady voice, grounding him with her words, instructing him to focus on his breathing. Slowly, his chest stopped heaving, and his breaths became deeper and more controlled. His body, once rigid with fear, gradually loosened.

His parents stood by, watching helplessly. His father ran a hand through his hair, his face etched with guilt. "It's my fault," he muttered, his voice heavy with regret.

Someone from the gathering placed a comforting hand on his shoulder and asked, "Why do you feel that way? What happened?"

Tears welled in his father's eyes as he spoke. "My son, Adveet, has social anxiety disorder. He struggles with being in crowds, with interacting, with even speaking sometimes. He avoids gatherings like this. But I thought... I thought if he faced it, maybe he'd get better. Maybe being around family would help. But I was wrong. It only made things worse."

His mother, tears streaming down her face, nodded. "We've been consulting professionals for a long time, but nothing seems to change. We just wanted to help him." The psychologist, Dr Aarohi looked at them with empathy. "Exposing him suddenly to a large crowd might not be the right approach. Social anxiety is complex, and forcing situations on him could intensify his fear instead of helping him overcome it. Healing takes time, patience, and the right strategies."

As the conversation unfolded, Adveet, now feeling better, re-joined his family. Though exhausted, he offered a small nod to his parents, letting them know he was okay. They quietly left the gathering and went back home, giving Adveet the space, he needed to recover.

As the gathering resumed, the atmosphere, once filled with joyful chatter, had shifted into something deeper. One person spoke about the stress at their workplace, the pressure eating away at their mental peace. Another shared their struggle with sleepless nights, anxiety creeping into their thoughts at odd hours. One by one, people started opening up. What began as a celebration turned into an eye-opening discussion about mental health, an issue often ignored or misunderstood.

Dr Aarohi seeing the shift in conversation, took the opportunity to speak. "Mental health is just as important as physical health," she began. "Yet, in our society, we often overlook it until it becomes too serious to ignore. Many people think therapy is unnecessary or a waste of money. Others believe seeking help is a sign of weakness. But that's far from the truth. Just as we go to a doctor for a physical illness, we need to seek professional help for mental health issues."

Someone from the crowd raised their hand hesitantly. "You mentioned stigma earlier. What exactly does that mean?"

Dr Aarohi smiled kindly. "Stigma refers to the negative attitudes and discrimination people face because of mental health issues. For example, if someone openly talks about their anxiety or depression, they might be labelled as weak or dramatic. In workplaces, people with mental health conditions may not get the same opportunities because they are seen as less capable. Some families even discourage seeking therapy, believing it will bring shame or that 'talking to a stranger won't help.' These beliefs prevent people from getting the help they need."

Another person chimed in, "I've seen people avoid therapy because they think it's too expensive. So, they go to untrained individuals who claim to 'fix' their problems for a lower cost."

Dr Aarohi nodded. "Yes, and that's a huge mistake. Mental health treatment should always come from trained professionals, licensed psychologists, psychiatrists, or therapists. Many people go to unqualified individuals who offer quick solutions. But instead of helping, these untrained people often make the condition worse, leading to deeper emotional damage.

Mental health professionals study for years to understand the complexities of the human mind. Just like you wouldn't go to an unqualified person for heart surgery, you shouldn't trust untrained people with your mental well-being."

The room was silent as her words sank in.

"We need to change how we see mental health. It's not something to be ashamed of. It's not something to hide. It's part of our overall well-being. Seeking help is not a sign of weakness; it's a sign of strength. We need to give it the same importance as we give to physical illnesses. Depression, anxiety, and stress are real issues, and they deserve real solutions. The more we talk about it, the more we break the stigma, and the more people will be willing to seek help without fear."

A wave of understanding swept through the gathering. Faces that had once been filled with concern now held a sense of awareness. The conversation had shifted from personal struggles to collective realization. Mental health mattered.

As the night came to an end, the family members embraced each other a little tighter. They left with more than just memories, they left with knowledge, with a newfound perspective on something that had been ignored for too long, in that old house, filled with generations of love, a new journey began, one of awareness, of breaking barriers, and of embracing mental health as an essential part of life.

9

The New Story

CHAPTER 1: The Unseen Battle

A sweet voice is whispering... It starts speaking softly,

"Once upon a time, there lived four characters named **Cortic, Critic, Echo, and Neuro**. They were inseparable, always present in the same space, influencing one another in ways unseen to the world. Though they coexisted, their relationships were far from harmonious.

Cortic, the thinker, appeared calm and composed on the outside, but internally, a storm raged. He constantly sought validation from Critic, the harsh judge, whose words made Cortic doubt his every move. Echo, the shadow of fear, whispered reminders of past failures, making Cortic even more hesitant. Neuro, the quiet but wise guide, remained in the background, patiently waiting for the moment when his voice would be heard."

Cortic opened his eyes to find himself in a vast, dimly lit cave. The air was thick, and the walls stretched endlessly in every direction. He wasn't alone, Critic stood beside him, looking unimpressed and irritated.

"Where are we?" Cortic asked, his voice laced with confusion.

Critic scoffed. "Isn't it obvious? This is where we belong. You got yourself trapped in your own mind again."

A chilling whisper echoed through the cave. "You'll never escape. This is your mind now."

Cortic shivered as the familiar voice of **Echo** slithered through the air. The words clung to him like a heavy weight. He knew Echo too well, always lurking, always waiting for the right moment to strike with doubt and fear.

"I don't remember how we got here," Cortic murmured, glancing around.

"That's because you never notice how deep you're sinking until it's too late," Critic sneered. "You let yourself overthink again. You always do."

Cortic's breath grew unsteady. Was Critic, right? Had he done this to himself? The cave felt suffocating, a reflection of the endless thoughts that overwhelmed him daily. He turned in desperation, hoping to find a way out.

That's when he saw it, a faint glow on the ground. A message, etched into the stone:

"The only way out is through."

Cortic knelt down, tracing the words with his fingers. "Who wrote this?"

"That would be me."

A calm, steady voice echoed through the cave. From the shadows emerged **Neuro**, his presence unlike the others. Where Echo brought fear and Critic brought judgment, Neuro brought something unfamiliar, clarity.

Cortic swallowed hard. "Through what?"

Neuro stepped closer; his expression unwavering. "Through the darkness, through the fear, through the uncertainty. The only way to escape this place is to confront what's inside it."

Critic crossed his arms. "Sounds ridiculous. Why should we listen to you?"

Neuro didn't waver. "Because I know the truth, you don't have to stay trapped. You just have to take the first step."

Cortic hesitated. Could he really trust Neuro? Or was this just another trick of his own mind? The cave loomed around him, dark and endless, as Echo's whispers grew louder.

To escape, Cortic had to make a choice.

The walls of the cave seemed to close in, shadows shifting with every passing second. The more Cortic hesitated, the louder Echo became.

"You're too weak to leave," Echo hissed. "Even if you try, you'll fail. You always do."

Cortic clenched his fists. He had heard those words before, many times. They felt real, but were they? His heart pounded as his mind swirled in confusion. The weight of his past failures, every mistake, every regret, stacked themselves against him like unscalable walls.

Critic stepped forward. "Maybe Echo's right. You've always struggled to make decisions. What if stepping forward makes things worse?"

Cortic looked at Neuro, searching for reassurance. Neuro remained calm, patient. "You don't have to silence them, Cortic," he said. "You just have to take a step despite them."

The words settled over Cortic like a faint warmth. He wasn't being asked to defeat Echo or argue with Critic, only to move forward. His hands trembled as he stood up, glancing at the message glowing beneath him once more.

The only way out is through.

Cortic took a deep breath and stepped forward.

The cave trembled. The darkness rippled, as though resisting his movement. Echo's whispers grew frantic, trying to pull him back. "You're making a mistake! Turn back now!"

But Cortic didn't stop. His feet carried him forward, step by step. The more he moved, the fainter the whispers became. He wasn't free yet, but something had changed.

Neuro walked beside him. "You're learning," he said. "Anxiety isn't about getting rid of fear. It's about walking forward, even when it follows you."

Cortic felt lighter. He wasn't completely free of the cave, but for the first time, he could see a path ahead.

And he was willing to take it.

Echoes of anxiety

CHAPTER 2: The Illusion of Control

(Overthinking vs. Taking Action)

Cortic stood still. His hands twitched at his sides, his mind racing faster than his body could move. The path ahead stretched into the unknown, and he hesitated.

"We need a plan before we move," he muttered. "We should analyse every possibility first."

Critic rolled his eyes. "You're doing it again," he said. "You're stuck, Cortic. You always do this, thinking, thinking, thinking, but never acting."

Cortic ignored him, staring at the dark tunnel before them. **What if it was the wrong path? What if there was danger ahead? What if he failed again?**

Echo's voice slithered into his mind. "What if you make the wrong choice?" it whispered. "You'll regret it. You always do."

The shadows of the cave flickered, closing in around him. **The longer he waited, the more impossible movement seemed.** The air grew heavy, pressing against his chest like an invisible weight. His thoughts tangled into knots, trapping him in his own fear.

Neuro stepped forward; his presence steady. "Cortic," he said gently. "Overthinking won't give you control. It only gives you fear."

"But what if,"

"No." Neuro's voice was firm. "You'll never have all the answers. You don't need them. You just need to move."

Cortic swallowed hard. The cave around him wasn't changing, **he was the one making it harder to move**. He exhaled slowly, lifting his foot off the ground.

Critic scoffed. "Finally."

Cortic stepped forward. The cave trembled again, but this time, he didn't let it stop him. He took another step, and then another. The more he moved, the lighter he felt.

Neuro nodded approvingly. "That's it. Control isn't about knowing everything. It's about trusting yourself enough to take the next step."

For the first time, Cortic felt like he was moving toward something, not away from it.

And he wasn't alone.

CHAPTER 3: The Voices Outside (Stigma & Misunderstanding of Anxiety)

As Cortic continued walking through the dimly lit tunnel, an unsettling sensation gripped his chest. It wasn't just the suffocating darkness pressing in on him, it was something heavier, something invisible yet tangible. Then he heard them.

Distant murmurs floated through the air, growing louder as he approached a vast, open space. The tunnel widened into an eerie expanse, where shadowy figures clustered in groups, their hushed whispers dripping with disdain.

At first, the words were indecipherable, merging into a low hum. But as Cortic took a hesitant step forward, the voices sharpened, their tones laced with condescension and impatience.

"Why are you even anxious? Just stop thinking about it," one scoffed.

"Anxiety is just overreacting. You're weak," another muttered, their voice tinged with scorn.

"It's all in your head. Just be happy!" someone else added, their dismissive tone twisting like a knife in Cortic's chest.

He froze. His pulse quickened; his breath shallowed. The words weren't new. They were echoes, echoes from the world outside his mind, words he had heard from friends, family, even strangers who had never understood. They had always dismissed his struggles, brushing aside his anxiety as though it were a mere inconvenience, a choice he could simply refuse.

And now, they stood before him, their whispers coiling around him like invisible chains.

Echo took the opportunity to lean in, his presence like a creeping shadow in Cortic's mind. His voice was a soft hiss, deceptively soothing. "See? Even they think you're broken."

Cortic lowered his head, shame crawling over him like a thick, suffocating fog. Maybe they were right. Maybe he was just weak.

Critic, the ever-watchful spectre of his deepest insecurities, stepped forward with a smirk. "You've always known the truth, haven't you?" His voice was smooth, dripping with quiet cruelty. "They wouldn't say it if it weren't true."

The words dug into Cortic's already fragile defences, unravelling every reassurance he had tried to build. Memories resurfaced, moments when he had confided in someone only to be met with eye-rolls or impatient sighs. The times when he had forced himself to act normal, to push through, only to be told he was being dramatic. Every dismissive comment, every misunderstanding, every invalidation piled onto his shoulders, pressing him down.

"You're exhausting to be around."

"You always make things harder than they need to be."

"Just get over it."

Each phrase stung like a lash, old wounds reopening. His hands trembled. His thoughts raced.

What if they were right?

What if he was just weak?

What if he was broken beyond repair?

Neuro's voice cut through the storm raging in his mind. It was steady, unwavering. "Cortic, don't listen to them."

Cortic clenched his fists. "But… what if they're right?" His voice was barely a whisper, heavy with doubt.

Neuro stepped beside him, his presence grounding. "They speak from ignorance, not truth. Anxiety isn't a choice. It isn't weakness. And you don't have to prove your struggle to anyone."

Cortic hesitated. The weight of those words, the weight of years spent believing those voices, wasn't so easy to shake. It was easier to believe the worst about himself than to challenge it.

"They see only what they want to see," Neuro continued. "They see reactions, not reasons. Symptoms, not struggles."

Cortic lifted his gaze slightly. The shadowy figures hadn't moved. They still whispered, still scoffed, still judged. But something shifted in his mind.

Maybe their words weren't truths.

Maybe they were just opinions.

Maybe their judgment said more about them than it did about him.

Taking a deep, shaky breath, Cortic stepped forward. The whispers did not stop, but he walked past them. The voices reached for him, their words still laced with poison, but they did not root him in place this time. He wasn't free yet. The battle was far from over. But for the first time, he had taken a step beyond the voices, and for now, that was enough.

CHAPTER 4: The Weight of "What If"

(Fear of the Future vs. Accepting the Present)

Cortic stepped forward, but the path ahead had vanished. The tunnel no longer guided him; instead, an expanse of darkness stretched before him, an endless void with no way across. His heart pounded. There was no way forward, no solid ground, no certainty.

Then, out of the emptiness, a bridge began to form.

It was fragile, swaying, barely holding together. The stones beneath his feet weren't sturdy rock but fragmented whispers, carved with the words "What If." Each stone flickered, uncertain, barely solidifying before another replaced it. The bridge was unstable, unreliable, shifting under the weight of hesitation.

Echo's voice slithered into his thoughts, growing louder, feeding on the uncertainty.

"What if we fail?"

The bridge trembled. Cortic's breath hitched.

"What if they all laugh at us?"

A stone beneath him cracked, sending a splintering echo into the void.

"What if nothing ever gets better?"

The entire bridge shuddered. The words weren't just fearing; they were weights dragging him down, pressing against his chest, squeezing the air from his lungs. He clutched his arms, frozen between terror and the unknown.

Critic appeared beside him, smirking as he always did. "Look at this pathetic excuse for a path," he sneered. "It won't hold. You know it won't. You should turn back before you fall."

Cortic swallowed hard. His legs felt like lead. His mind screamed at him to retreat, to find another way, to stay where he was because at least here, he knew what to expect.

But another voice spoke, softer, but steady.

Neuro; "The future is uncertain, Cortic. That doesn't mean it's doomed."

Cortic's hands trembled. "But what if,"

Neuro cut him off gently. "What if you make it?"

Cortic hesitated. His mind had always filled in the blanks with disaster, weaving catastrophe out of uncertainty. But what if, just for a moment, he allowed himself to believe something else?

Taking a slow, shaky breath, he lifted his foot. The bridge groaned beneath him, but it did not break. He took another step. Then another.

The whispers didn't stop. The stones still trembled. But he was moving.

Because uncertainty was survivable, and for now, that was enough.

CHAPTER 5: The Stigma Gate (Facing Judgment & Breaking Free)

The path led Cortic to a towering structure, a massive gate stretching high into the darkness above. Its surface was cold, metallic, and unyielding, etched with rusted words that bled into the shadows: Fear. Shame. Weakness.

He reached out hesitantly, pressing his palm against the surface. The moment he touched it; laughter erupted from behind him. Familiar. Cruel.

Critic and the shadowy figures emerged from the gloom, their voices dripping with mockery.

"You should be able to handle this alone."

The gate rumbled; the words carved into it glowing faintly as if absorbing the weight of their judgment.

"Therapy is for the weak ones."

The glow intensified, the gate locking itself tighter.

Cortic's chest tightened. He had heard these words before, spoken with disappointment, with dismissal, with the implication that struggle was failure, that needing help was shameful. The weight of those beliefs pressed down on him, making his legs feel like stone.

Echo leaned in, whispering, "They'll never understand. You'll always be seen as broken."

Critic smirked. "If you go through that gate, they'll judge you forever."

Cortic's fingers curled into fists. The gate loomed before him, unmovable, unrelenting. Was it even possible to pass through? Was there another way? Or was he meant to stand here, forever trapped by fear of what others thought?

Then, Neuro's voice cut through the noise, steady, unwavering.

"Not everyone will understand. Walk through anyway."

Cortic inhaled sharply.

Not everyone would understand.

Not everyone had to.

He didn't need permission to heal. He didn't need validation to move forward. The gate wasn't keeping him locked in, his fear was.

Taking a deep breath, he stepped forward. The laughter grew louder, the words on the gate flaring with intensity. But this time, they didn't stop him.

He pressed his hands against the metal again. It was cold, but no longer unbearable. The words carved into its surface flickered… then faded.

With a deep, echoing groan, the gate slowly swung open.

Critic's smirk faltered.

Cortic stepped through. He was still healing. Still learning. But he was free.

CHAPTER 6: The Shadow's Trick (Intrusive Thoughts vs. Reality)

The air thickened as Cortic stepped forward. The path ahead dimmed, and the shadows around him deepened, coiling like living things. He could feel something shifting in the darkness, something watching. Then, the shadows stirred. They gathered, twisted, and rose, taking shape.

A figure emerged.

It was neither solid nor entirely formless, a dark mass that flickered and shifted like smoke caught in a storm. Its edges wavered, blurring between shapes, sometimes monstrous, sometimes familiar. It had no face, yet Cortic felt its eyes on him.

Then, it spoke.

Its voice was his own.

"If you ignore me, I'll get louder."

Cortic tensed. The voice wasn't just echoing in the air; it was inside him, crawling through his thoughts. He had always tried to silence these fears, to push them down, to pretend they weren't there. But the more he ignored them, the more they clawed their way back, stronger, sharper, suffocating.

The Shadow swirled, growing larger. Its form darkened, looming over him.

"What if something terrible happens?" it whispered.

Cortic's breath hitched.

"What if you lose control?"

The Shadow surged forward. The world around him shrank, the air tightening like invisible hands wrapping around his lungs.

"What if you never get better?"

The words struck deep, wrapping around his mind like chains. His body trembled. His heartbeat pounded in his ears. He wanted to run, to escape, to do anything to make it stop.

But there was nowhere to go.

The Shadow grew, feeding on his panic.

And then,

A thought. A quiet, fragile thought.

Cortic had always fought these moments. He had always tried to force them away. But what if… he didn't?

He took a shaky breath. His hands clenched and unclenched at his sides. He forced himself to look at the Shadow, really look at it. It was terrifying, but was it real?

Or was it just a trick?

His pulse still raced, his chest still felt tight, but he whispered, "These are just thoughts."

The Shadow flickered.

"They feel real," Cortic admitted, his voice barely above a breath. "But that doesn't mean they are real."

The Shadow wavered. It shrank, its edges fraying, its darkness thinning. The whispers didn't vanish, but they softened, losing their grip.

Cortic exhaled slowly.

The fear was still there. The thoughts still came. But they were not truths, just echoes of fear, just passing clouds in his mind's sky.

And if he could see through them, they could no longer control him.

The Shadow shrank further, curling into itself, until it was nothing more than a whisper on the wind.

Cortic took a step forward, his mind a little clearer.

The thoughts would come again.

But now, he knew he didn't have to believe them.

CHAPTER 7: The Wall of Perfection (Breaking Free from Unrealistic Expectations)

The path ahead seemed clear, until it wasn't.

A massive wall loomed before Cortic, stretching so high it seemed to disappear into the darkened sky. Its surface was smooth, impossibly polished, yet etched into it were sharp, unforgiving words: Not Enough. Failure. Weak. Disappointment.

Cortic's stomach twisted as he ran his fingers along the cold stone. The words weren't just carved into the wall, they were carved into him. Every expectation he had failed to meet, every mistake he had made, every standard he had fallen short of, standing before him in physical form.

He clenched his jaw. "We can't move forward unless we do everything perfectly."

The wall stood firm, unmoving, unbreakable.

Echo stirred in the shadows, his voice slithering through the cracks of doubt. "If you don't do it perfectly, why bother at all?"

Critic stepped beside him, arms crossed, smirking. "People expect excellence. You'll only embarrass yourself if you try and fail."

Cortic's fists tightened. He had spent so much of his life striving, pushing, chasing perfection like a mirage in the desert, never quite reaching it, yet always feeling like he should be able to. Every misstep, every flaw felt like proof that he wasn't enough.

His breathing quickened. There was no way around the wall, no way over it. He would be stuck here forever unless,

Unless he was perfect.

But then… a thought emerged, unsteady but insistent.

What if this wall wasn't as real as it seemed?

He hesitated, pressing his palm against the stone once more. The surface was cold but… was it solid? Or was it built from something else, something more fragile than he had believed?

Neuro's voice was quiet but firm. "Perfection isn't the price of progress, Cortic. You built this wall. And you can bring it down."

Cortic swallowed hard. "But if I fail,"

"You will. And you'll learn. And you'll move forward anyway."

He stood there, staring at the words carved into the wall. They still stung. The fear of failure still clawed at his chest. But maybe… just maybe… he didn't have to obey it.

He exhaled slowly and took a step forward, not to climb, not to break through, but to let go.

The wall trembled.

Another step.

The cracks spread, splintering through the impossible expectations, through the weight of years spent believing perfection was the only way forward.

And then,

The wall crumbled.

The words shattered into dust, dissolving into the wind.

The path was open again. And for the first time, he realized,

He didn't need to be perfect to keep going.

CHAPTER 8: The Exit, Or a New Beginning?

(Managing Anxiety Instead of Fighting It)

Cortic had lost track of how long he had been walking. The tunnels, the voices, the fears, they had all felt endless. But now, the path stretched ahead into an open space, bathed in a soft, unfamiliar glow. There, at the far end, stood a door.

The exit.

His heart pounded. He should feel relieved. He had fought his way through every challenge, confronted his fears, torn down the walls that had once imprisoned him. Yet as he took a step closer, a strange hesitation gripped him. Was this truly an escape? Or was it something else?

A presence stirred beside him. Neuro.

"The final challenge," he murmured. "But this one isn't about fighting."

Cortic glanced at him, confused. "Then what is it about?"

Neuro's expression was calm. "Acceptance."

A familiar whisper curled in the air. Echo.

"Acceptance?" the voice scoffed. "So, you're just supposed to live with this? With me?"

The shadows around them flickered, remnants of old fears still lingering. Cortic swallowed hard. He had spent so long battling his anxiety, treating it as an enemy, trying to silence it, trying to defeat it. But had he ever really won? Or had he only exhausted himself, always waiting for the next wave, the next attack, the next moment of uncertainty?

"The cave was never the enemy," Neuro said softly. "It was your mind all along."

Cortic exhaled.

It was true, wasn't it? The cave, the fears, the walls, the voices, it had all come from within. He had been fighting himself this entire time. And the more he fought, the more lost he became.

Anxiety wasn't something he could destroy. It wasn't something he could outrun. But maybe… he didn't have to.

He took another step forward, but this time, it wasn't to escape. It was to understand.

The door stood before him now, solid and real. He reached for the handle, but before turning it, he glanced back. The cave behind him hadn't disappeared. The tunnels still stretched into darkness; the whispers still murmured in the distance.

And yet, he wasn't afraid anymore.

"The cave will always be there," Neuro said. "But now, you know how to navigate it."

Cortic nodded.

Anxiety would always be a part of him. The thoughts, the doubts, the fears, they wouldn't vanish. But they didn't have to control him. He could move forward, not by erasing them, but by learning to live alongside them.

With a steady breath, he turned the handle and stepped through the door.

Not an exit.

A beginning.

As he stepped through, he found himself standing in a vast, open field bathed in golden light. The air was fresh, the horizon endless. The weight he had carried for so long felt lighter, not gone, but manageable. He could still hear the echoes of his fears, but they were distant now, like waves in the background rather than a storm engulfing him.

Neuro walked beside him. "There will still be difficult days, but you've learned something important. You don't have to fight every thought. You don't have to prove anything. You only have to keep moving forward."

Cortic closed his eyes for a moment, letting the realization settle in. He had spent so much time trying to find an exit, a way to make his anxiety disappear forever. But that was never the goal.

The goal was to live.

He inhaled deeply, feeling the warmth of the sun on his skin, the solid ground beneath his feet. He had faced the darkness. He had walked through the cave.

And now, he was ready for whatever lay ahead.

CHAPTER 9: The New Path

(Facing the Monster)

Cortic had thought the journey was over when he stepped through the door, but beyond it, a new challenge awaited. The golden light of the open field had been deceiving, because in the distance, something loomed. A monstrous shadow, towering and shapeless, shifting with every flicker of doubt.

The final test.

Neuro stood beside him, steady as always. "You knew this moment would come."

Cortic swallowed hard. He had expected to leave his fears behind, but here they were, waiting for him in a form more terrifying than ever. A swirling storm of every worry, every cruel whisper, every impossible standard he had held himself to. And at the core of it, Critic and Echo, their voices woven into the very fabric of the beast.

"You thought you were free?" Critic's voice hissed, slithering through the air. "You really believe you've changed?"

Echo's voice followed, softer but sharper. "The past doesn't just disappear. What if you're still the same? What if this feeling won't last?"

The monster's form twisted, its dark tendrils reaching out, curling toward him like claws.

For a moment, fear locked him in place. His old instincts screamed at him to run, to fight, to do anything to make this feeling stop. But something was different this time.

He wasn't alone.

Neuro placed a hand on his shoulder. "Cortic, what happens if you don't run?"

Cortic inhaled shakily. What happens if he doesn't run? If he doesn't fight? If he just… stands there and lets it be?

The monster growled, shifting again, its form flickering with memories,

The time he had stayed awake all night, replaying an awkward conversation over and over, convinced he had embarrassed himself beyond repair.

The moment he had almost spoken up in class but stopped himself, fearing judgment more than he craved understanding.

The days he had spent trapped in his own thoughts, convincing himself he wasn't good enough, wasn't strong enough, wasn't enough.

Every moment of doubt, of self-hatred, of overwhelming anxiety, this monster was built from all of it. And yet…

Cortic took a deep breath. "I see you."

The monster hesitated.

"I hear you." He took a step forward. "I've spent so much of my life fighting you, fearing you. But I understand now."

The monster trembled. The shadows flickered, uncertain.

"You are my anxiety." Cortic's voice grew steadier. "You are my fears. You are Echo and Critic. But you are not me."

A pause. Then, a shift.

The monster's tendrils recoiled, not out of anger, but something else. Uncertainty? Weakness? It had thrived on his fear, his resistance. But now? Now he was stepping closer.

And then, he did the one thing he had never done before.

He reached out.

The moment his fingers met the darkness, the monster let out a shuddering breath. The shadows rippled. The growling stopped. The twisted form began to shrink, unravelling into threads of mist. Echo and Critic's voices faded into a whisper, still present, but no longer overwhelming.

Cortic closed his eyes. "You don't define me anymore."

When he opened them again, the monster was gone.

The path ahead was clear.

Neuro smiled. "You faced it. You didn't run. And now, you can move forward."

For the first time, Cortic felt something new in his chest, something lighter, something freer. He had always believed that conquering his fears meant making them disappear. But now, he understood the truth.

Anxiety would always be a part of his journey. Echo and Critic might always whisper. The shadows might still lurk in the corners of his mind. But he was no longer controlled by them.

He turned toward the new path, feeling the warmth of the sun on his face. With Neuro beside him, he stepped forward, his heart lighter than it had ever been.

This wasn't just an ending,

CHAPTER 10: Embracing the journey
(Moving forward)

Cortic took one last step forward, the warmth of the sun washing over him. The dark cave, the twisting Cave, the monstrous shadows, they were all behind him now. He had walked through fear, faced his doubts, and something deep within him had shifted. The weight that had once pressed on his chest felt lighter, as if he had finally loosened the chains that held him down.

Neuro stood beside him, watching as Cortic inhaled deeply, filling his lungs with air that no longer felt so suffocating.

"You did it," Neuro said softly.

Cortic turned to him, a small but genuine smile forming on his lips. "I didn't fight the fear," he realized. "I accepted it."

Neuro nodded. "Fear loses its power when you stop running from it."

For the first time, Cortic didn't feel the need to look over his shoulder, to check if the shadows were still lurking. He knew they would always be there, whispering from the edges of his mind, but they no longer dictated his path. He was walking forward, not to escape, but to live.

As he and Neuro stepped onto the new path, the golden light around them grew brighter, washing everything in a sense of peace. The journey wasn't over. It never truly would be. But now, Cortic had something he never had before.

Hope.

Finally, that sweet voice: come-on take a deep breath and slowly open your eyes...

Adveet exhaled sharply, his fingers twitching against the fabric of the chair.

The warmth of the golden sun faded. The sounds of the open field disappeared. The cave, the Cave, the voices, all of it dissolved like mist being carried away by the wind.

And then…

He was back.

The soft light of Dr Aarohi's office greeted him. The walls were lined with books, the scent of lavender lingering in the air. He felt the cushion of the chair beneath him, the rhythmic ticking of the clock in the background grounding him to reality.

His breath was steady. His hands weren't clenched into fists. He blinked slowly, as if his mind was adjusting to where he truly was.

Dr Aarohi sat across from him, her warm eyes studying him with patience. She tilted her head slightly, the way she always did when she was waiting for him to process his thoughts.

"How do you feel?" she finally asked.

Adveet parted his lips, but no words came at first. He had been somewhere else entirely, trapped inside his mind, lost within the metaphorical journey she had guided him through. But now, he was here, fully present, and something inside him had shifted.

"I feel…" He searched for the right word. "Lighter."

Dr Aarohi smiled. "Good. You faced it."

Adveet nodded, letting the weight of those words sink in. You faced it.

For so long, he had feared social situations, worried about judgment, convinced that he would always be trapped inside his own mind. But today, he had walked through that fear. He had seen the voices for what they were, just voices. Just thoughts. And thoughts didn't have to define him.

Before he could say anything else, the door to the office creaked open. His parents stepped in, their expressions cautious but hopeful. His mother's eyes scanned his face, searching for any sign of distress, but as she took in his calm demeanour, relief flooded her features.

His father cleared his throat. "Last time, you helped him through a tough time," he said to Dr Aarohi, his voice filled with gratitude. "And today… we could see it in his face the moment we walked in. This therapy, this journey, it's making a difference."

Adveet met his mother's gaze, then his father's. He saw something in their eyes that he hadn't noticed before, not just concern, but pride. They weren't just relieved. They were proud of him.

His mother turned to Dr Aarohi, her voice slightly trembling with emotion. "Ma'am, I can't tell you how grateful we are. That day… if you hadn't been there, we don't know how we would've handled it. Adveet wouldn't even step out of his room, let alone come to a gathering. And now, seeing him like this…" She wiped a tear from the corner of her eye. "Thank you for asking us to visit your clinic again. Without you, I don't think we would have made it here today."

His father nodded. "We thought we had lost him to his fears, that maybe this was just how things were going to be. But you showed us that there was another way. You gave us hope."

Dr Aarohi gave a gentle smile. "Adveet did the work. I only guided him. And this is just the beginning." She turned to Adveet. "You're learning to carry your anxiety in a way that doesn't control you. That is real progress."

Adveet took a deep breath, feeling those words settle in his chest. He wasn't healed overnight. He still had a long way to go. But he understood something now.

Anxiety wasn't the enemy. It wasn't something to defeat or destroy. It was simply a part of him, one that he could learn to live with, to manage, to walk beside rather than run from.

As he stepped outside the clinic, the world felt a little brighter. The air was crisp, the sounds of the city alive around him. People passed by, chatting, laughing, living their lives. And for the first time in a long time, Adveet didn't feel so out of place among them.

He wasn't escaping anymore. He was moving forward.

A FINAL REFLECTION

Cortic – The Worrier

Cortic represents the **cortex**, the part of the brain responsible for decision-making, reasoning, and overanalysing. It also symbolizes **cortisol**, the hormone associated with stress and anxiety. This is the voice of overthinking the one that questions every action, dissects every possibility, and amplifies the worst-case scenarios. Cortic thrives on anxiety, creating an endless loop of doubt and hesitation, making even simple choices feel overwhelming. Often, Cortic listens to **Echo**, believing every fear and hesitation to be true, leading to spirals of worry and indecision.

Critic – The External Judgment

The embodiment of **society's dismissiveness and stigma**, Critic represents external pressures and societal expectations. It is the voice that reminds people of how they are perceived, enforcing the idea that struggles should be hidden rather than addressed. Critic echoes judgmental glances, unrealistic standards, and the stigma surrounding mental health, reinforcing shame and self-doubt. Many times, people suffer under **Critic's** influence, fearing that seeking help will make them appear weak.

Echo – The Shadow of Doubt

Named after the **echo phenomenon**, which refers to involuntary repetition, Echo represents **intrusive thoughts** that replay endlessly in the mind. This is the voice of self-doubt, regret, and fear, the one that replays past mistakes, distorts reality, and makes anxieties feel like undeniable truths. Echo traps individuals in a loop of negative thinking, making it difficult to break free from self-sabotage. When Cortic listens too closely to Echo, overthinking intensifies, making even the smallest problems seem insurmountable.

Neuro – The Guide to Healing

Inspired by **neuroplasticity**, the brain's ability to change and adapt, Neuro is the voice of **self-awareness and growth**. Unlike the others, Neuro does not create fear, it offers guidance. This voice encourages resilience, reminding individuals that healing is possible. Neuro represents the power of therapy, self-compassion, and emotional strength, providing the tools needed to overcome internal struggles. Neuro's messages help **Cortic** take control, showing that anxiety isn't about elimination, it's about adaptation. By acknowledging Neuro's wisdom, one can learn to quiet Echo's doubts and stand strong against Critic's judgments.

These voices exist within everyone, shaping thoughts, emotions, and decisions. Some voices create fear and hesitation, while others guide toward healing and self-discovery. Understanding them is the first step in navigating mental health challenges.

To the Reader:

Anxiety is not a battle you have to fight alone. Like Adveet, like Cortic, you may face moments of darkness, of self-doubt, of fear that seems impossible to overcome. But you are not weak for feeling this way. You are not broken.

It's okay to struggle. It's okay to ask for help. Seeking therapy, talking to loved ones, or simply taking small steps toward healing doesn't make you weak, it makes you courageous.

Healing is a journey, not a destination. And every step forward, no matter how small, is a victory.

So, take a deep breath.

Step forward.

You are capable of more than you believe. And you are never, ever alone.

"Anxiety isn't a prison—it's a lock you've always had the key to."

About the Author – Bhoomika Madhusudhan

Bhoomika Madhusudhan is a writer and mental health profession with a Master's degree in Clinical Psychology. Passionate about understanding the complexities of the human mind, she is a keen observer of human emotions and behaviour. She has always been fascinated by the intricate ways in which thoughts and feelings shape our lives. With a deep-rooted belief in the power of storytelling, Bhoomika aims to create narratives that not only engage but also provide solace to those navigating their own mental health journeys.

Writing has been a part of her life for as long as she can remember, but this book holds a special place in her heart. It marks her first published work—a step toward her lifelong dream of making a meaningful impact through words. She hopes that readers will find a sense of understanding, connection, and hope within these pages.

Beyond writing, Bhoomika enjoys delving into psychological research, engaging in mindfulness practices, and spreading awareness about mental health. She strongly believes that healing is not about eliminating fear but about learning to walk alongside it with courage and acceptance.

www.ingramcontent.com/pod-product-compliance
Lightning Source LLC
Chambersburg PA
CBHW020501160726
47991CB00007B/2764